With a Mouse (to your Mouth)

I0672265

Nick Peterson

DEDICATION

TO WHOM IT MAY CONCERN

ISBN 9780990857044 © 2024 Nick Peterson - Old Nick   and published by DiaryUnlimited an Imprint of The Edge Press. All rights reserved. AnotherClip.com

Contents

Dramatis Personae

AI - Narrator
X1 - Old Nick
X2 (X1's alter ego)
X3 (X1's alter ego multiplied when things are going out of control)
Y-X1 - Thus called in Y++
Y-X2 - Thus called in Y++
JD - Jane D'Arbanville, X1 imaginary girlfriend
A girl by the river in In and Out of Planet Earth
Sir Y
Lady Y
Junior Virus 2 a
Junior Virus 2 b
Junior Virus 3 a
Cohorts of viruses 1: K-1, K-2, K-3, K-4, K-5, K-6, K-7, K-8, K-9.
Cohorts of viruses 2: P-1, P-2, P-3, P-4, P-5, P-6, P-7, P-8, P-9.
Cohorts of Super Amoebas: A-1 to A-100.
God

1010101010101010101010101010101010101010

Prologue

X1

This is the list of characters from this film. The film is an exploration of the state of the brain when it is infected by a horde of germs and viruses.
A mouse enters the mouth and becomes a virus entering the human body.

The Zones

Zone A (Outside) and Zone B (Inside)

X1

This is the story of X. X is a little germ entering someone's mouth. X's vision is somewhat blurred. Its vision is in 'distorted 3D'. The mouth is the ultimate frontier between the inside of a creature and the rest of the universe. It is the border control. There is a long process before reaching the heart of the body. X aims to reproduce itself into the heart of the body just like a little mouse. When inside the body, X the germ can see, feel and breathe exactly what the creature's body sees, feels and breathes. It's often thrown out randomly. To be a germ is the ultimate fulfilment like a multiple orgasm.

A germ can dictate and control a whole body and there is very little anyone can do.'

Exhibit 1: ENTER

X1

'The colour is an impression, a visual sensation made upon the eye by the different light in contact with its surroundings resulting from the interpretation of the brain of the wavelength of perceived light, which enables one to differentiate between alternative identical objects. The primitive colours are the fundamental colours of the spectrum: red, orange, yellow, green, blue, indigo and violet. There are also the Simple Ones, the absence of colours that complement the spectrum seen in terms of hue, lightness and saturation, a degree mixing with white, grey or black. Felt simultaneously they give the impression of black and white.

There are also the four colours used in the printing process, in *quadrichromy*. Combined together, creating the illusion of a full colour painting or photography; CMYK -cyan, magenta, yellow and black.

These are similar to some extent to the one used by Stone Age artists. They had four colours to work with: red, yellow, brown and black. Combining two minerals: manganese oxide for black and iron oxide for the other colours. They were mixed together with water before being applied with fingers or with brushes, pads or crayons.

Without colours, we can't see, without colours, we don't exist without colours, we're timeless. Colours bring the illusion that we exist. In real life we can't see. In real life, there are no colours.

The whole story started somehow, on a rainy day watching some snails slipping slowly over the grass. Through the entire shape of a snail's life, we can see the features of his most primitive existence; the animal which symbolises the long achievement of time.

Time and life were passing slowly over the grass and time itself disappeared, the rainy sky moved into sunny day making the way to the night falling slowly over the grass.

Life is but a labyrinth where anyone should find his way out. No danger ceases; neither from inside nor the outside. No matter how long it could take, the most important thing is to find the key and never give up in doing so.

This is a story of time and life illustrated by a myth where time no longer exists; time being life and life being time. Life only exists in our imagination.   Time has only been created so that humans won't have to be afraid of emptiness.

Another crucial element is that blood circulates on a constant loop. It's just like watching a mouse turning in a circle, around and around, again and again.

When some germs die, it's rare but it happens. One dies and another million germs invade another body.

ZONE A

We're in 1995. X1 and his alter ego X2 are on a journey across London inside a black cab. X2 and X1 are reading to each other a book. It's the story of X the germ.

X1 and X2 are singing inside the cab.

X1 and X2

Confide in me,

Do you trust me?

And when I let you down?

Beat me, for I'm the mouse.

Need a shoulder to lean on?

Lonely or tired?

Need a crush to flip?

You're not inspired!

And when your best friend annoys you?

You tell it all

Meaningless fool

I pout and listen

Never will you know

Why do they hate you so...?

X1

ZONE B

X2

Hi. I'm X2. I'm from London, England. The
year is now 2002. But you may read these lines
way into the future. I've collected a series of
notes and decided to airmail them to the web.
It's the story of my alter ego, X1. One day,
inside a cab in London, he confided in me the
journey he went to during a coma, the result of
a road accident. I believe that by the time you'll
be reading these lines, I'll be dead, for about
fifty years or even one hundred years and
unlike my alter ego X1 still around somewhere

in time, in his mid-twenties.

I remember studying about the 1- or 2-bit display of the first PCs; Well, this is exactly how I and X2, my alter ego. We are 2 little dots, 2 little binary entities in black and white. Rather white out of black for that matter. Space never felt so empty. Bit-ting (and byt-ing) along, off the beaten track, hither drifting further on, we computed ourselves. Another dot peered into the horizon, and more dots seemed to dot my silhouette up.   Sound soon became an integrated part of the information technology as I could hear some noises reverberating from the dots shaping in the horizon.

X2 and X1 are wandering about in a different dimension, time and space. There is a beautiful tableau here, almost a pristine painting of red colour. Two white dots are moving about in the horizon. A conversation is being heard. The more voices are being heard and the more colours seem to be appearing, often merging in perfect transition.

X2

How do we navigate there?

X1

Surprise, surprise! I don't know enough. After all there aren't any doors or outstanding partitions to distinguish one from the other.

X2

The colours seem to move from one to another as we talk about them, on the other hand the colours are what we are making out of them. They evolve as long as they evolve to a time when our time has come and merged so that we could become a full part of it and just become a stain in the decor.'

X1

I shiver with anticipation, I demand blue!

X2

There is no need to shout. Blue is what you're getting anyway.

X1

Good, isn't it? Shall we have magenta then? Cyan, Green, turquoise...

X2

Stop! You're driving me mad. Grab one colour, make your life in it and let it become your reality.

X1

What did you say?

X2

Stick to one colour. Let that colour become your reality.' **Pause**. 'Anyway, I got you in the end!

X1

More the other way around...

X2

How can it be the other way around?

X1

'I've returned!

X2

Maybe...

X1

Surely

X2

Look: let's not argue about it, shall we?

X1

I suppose not...

X2

I've met you, right?

X1

...Right, er, yes you did!

X2

You look rather pale...

X1

So, do you...

X2

'Had a nice time then?'

X1

I'm not sure. It was the future.

Whilst continuing their little chat, they are slowly moving on forward -wherever that is-. Another group of 2 dots is seen on the top left-

hand side. The two dots in the centre are growing slowly until they both merge into each other to finally recover the screen.

X2

I brought some people along

X1

Made some friends, have you?

X2

'I'm not sure. It's in the future.

They have reached the end. It seems like a big wall, it's hard and it hurts when pushed into. They push, push and push harder. The wall collapses fragmented into thousands of little debris.

After the majestic fall of the wall X1, the Lady Y of the future, X1's alter ego X2 and the Sir Y of the future are assembled for a little gathering.

Sir Y

So, if we're no longer in the future, who am I?

Lady Y

You'll still be the same just like me. Sir Y, that is…

Sir Y

That's what I meant

Lady Y

We are still 2 scientists. We know what we are, what we were and what we would become. '

Sir Y

"We know the map of the universe but there is still a big Y missing. '

At this point, X2 can't stop himself. He has to interfere and looks at Sir Y straight into his eyes.

X2

And what would that be?

Sir Y

The Y is still turning around and around

Lady Y

Does it frighten you?

X2

Not as long as it is still running.

X1

Good on you X2 I think you've got it at last!

X1 thinks he won his point about proving his theory of life transportation.

X1

I won the argument, though. I have dragged them along from the future. They couldn't have done it by themselves. Not in a million years! I did it by myself. I'm the one who went to the future. They have never been able to do that and they are scientists from the future. Now, I've brought them back to the present. So, they are simple humans now, dragging their old carcass along with them. Just like everybody else in this world. Anyway; it proves my point. If I did it, anyone can do it.   They couldn't have done it as a scientist from the future; but as it is, as a simple human...I was a threat to them in the future because I knew, I knew it somehow. I had that knowledge about what they didn't know. But now we are here. So, I'm now no longer a threat to them. There you go...

X2

Hmm… But I also won the argument

X1

In which way

X2

I caught up with you. I've tracked you down through the net in the future. I brought you back to the present, to the past. I don't really know what happened but I found you on my screen and then I crashed. There was a white smoke everywhere and then it turned black and I found that I couldn't breathe. I tried to get away, and then ran off.

X2 is trying hard to remember. He re-starts his story.

X2

I tracked you down in the past and brought you back to the present. I'm not exactly sure what happened.   There was an explosion. There was all this white smoke and then it turned black and I found I couldn't breathe.   I tried to get away from it. I tried to run and then I fell. Then it was deadly cold. There was froth on my fingertips.   And then the cold went and the smoke cleared and I found I could breathe again.   When I blew on my hands, I couldn't feel the air. It was pitch black and I wandered through the dark, I don't know, maybe for hours and I heard talking. It was nothing I heard before. It was like a new language, a reverberated sound. It was very fast and I couldn't understand it. There was a white dot, a head and I followed it. I heard someone speaking and I knew it was you because I could understand you loud and clear.

Exhibit 2: MULTIPLY

X1

ZONE B

1. Upwards inside the brain. The muscles of the brain are the busiest in the whole body.

They need. They want. They demand.

2. Left side of the brain: very arty the little grey cells; nothing to report.

3. Right side: a right mess. A right dump. This is the thought process; desperately seeking to express a point of view. I must paralyse the beggar.   It should really be made illegal to think.

4. Centre-stage; the nerve centre directing the whole body. Lazy, dirty. Desperate.
Addicted. Always ready for the wrong move.

5. Rear-end. Trying too hard to be clever. The best place on this side of the world to lay down a few eggs.

6. Exit the brain. Corridor South. Must paralyse that blood tube all the way to the nervous system. It stinks here. It's like inside an animal rendering farm.

7. Down. East End. Corrosion. Rotten pipes. Fat: lots of it. No need to infect. Already collapsing by itself. Self-destruction is more like it.

8. As I glide scantily on the corridor to the Southern hemisphere, I'm bumping into other germs. Not one of the species I have been acquainted with before.

9. I try to contact one of the indigenes. Oh fuck. This guy is hitting on me. Ram Cinderella! Fancy that! Mistaken for a female!

10. Guilty on the non-reproduction front. I've been lazy. There is no doubt about it. I need a female now.

11. Slouching at throat level. I have just been to the toilets. This means this body will get a throat infection for a while. And I don't mean a little sore throat. We're talking full angina here.

My excrements are in full order.

12. I love my job. Deeper and deeper into the throat, entering some remote organs; whatever organ it is. It tastes absolutely delicious.

13. Slouching and going to the toilets again. As nature intended, at liver level. This should paralyse this organ for a bit.

14. I must stop eating and reproduce. At this rate I'll never be able to bequeath my legacy to this new Nation of mine.

15. Someone is doing a lot of banging down below. What is this? Some kind of a nightclub?

16. It is the heart. There were a lot of people there. It's all hallucinogenic here. What a crowd! Hey, I have been hijacked!

17. I'm squashed. Drained. Sucked. Syphoned and seeded. It has never happened to me before. On entering the mouth of this body, I was a male mouse, or I thought I was. Now I'm not sure anymore. It's gender-bending in this dump.

18. I've copulated. I'm in full bloom. Full of eggs. I'm reproducing. There is a thick flood of Yellowish water coming my way.

19. What a fine mess! I'm stuck on the lungs now. I'm about to burst. I feel so heavy. So full. It's all coming out now.

20. One, two, three, four then multiply by 10. By 100. By 1000. I can't even count all my children.

21. I have achieved the miracle of life. I've conceived an army of viruses. Ready to ransack that already self-obliterated lung. Gosh it's so dark in there.

22. Lunch. In the South.   Then "evacuation" in the South East. The toilet facilities are always impeccable in that region. Finally, a nap further East.

23. What a hullabaloo. An explosion of blood is overfilling the oesophagus. What the hell is going on?

24. My chance to get into the bloodstream. This river will get me to it.

25. Blood is a perfect nest to germinate. Procreate if you like. Seeds can flow inside like no tomorrow.

26. I'm about to burst again. One. Two. Three. My baby. My babies. A hundred. A thousand. One hundred thousand. Nothing like a blood stream. Deep penetration.

Exhibit 3: BRAIN CONTROL

X1

27. There are entire families of viruses. We can engage in pro-creation with most. Some we can't. It's hard to explain. It has always been like that. It's a non-ending cycle.

28. Some viruses are called artificial as they are a blend of man-made viruses. We can detect them from a mile away. The danger zones.

29. These humans who believe they have isolated 'a' virus or most viruses are always wrong. It is impossible to categorise different families of viruses as they evolve faster than what the humans are calling the 'speed of light'.

30. Of course, as a virus we know them all. We are the viruses. That's not a concept, the humans can understand.

31. Humans believe they can kill viruses. Humans believe many things. It makes them feel better.   A virus never dies.

32. Viruses can be silent. Silent for centuries, even millennia. Viruses may seem to have been killed. Viruses can't die. Viruses hibernate. When the time comes, viruses are ready to strike.

33. In human's count there are over a billion families of viruses; too many for them to keep a tab on our people.

34. Viruses know who they are and how many they are. It goes far beyond human's comprehension.

35. I was inside a mouse before and technically I was the mouse. I was in full control of the animal. I came out into the air and went straight into contact with a human mouth.

36. I entered this body through the mouth; my life is here inside now. I'm this human. I'm in control. He's a lucky human. I'm often very lazy. This guy's in it for the long haul.

37. I'm a master virus. All viruses reproduce by themselves. I do too. The difference between a master virus and an ordinary virus is that they can't copulate with other families, we can.

38. There are not many of us, master viruses in this world. We can't reproduce a master virus. We were born that way, once upon a time. No viruses know why or how. It's just like that.

39. Master viruses fear nothing. Ordinary viruses tend to be timid at times. They need the help of a master virus to fight an attack from the humans.

40. It may take a while to counter-attack and foil any human intervention. In the end, we always win the war. But wars are wars. They can linger on for years and be extremely messy.'

Exhibit 4: ATTACK FROM THE OUTSIDE

X1

41. Wars are "big business". Wars are games where master viruses excel in supreme intelligence. It's never easy. It's never simple.

42. Wars are always different yet there are some similarities. Of course, a virus leads a normal life. We do not foresee or even expect a war. It happens when it happens and we deal with it accordingly.

43. There are about 500 thousand of year 1 viruses in each body and 500 million older viruses.

44. There are about 1000 species of viruses, 100 different families. No one knows each other.

45. The master virus -that's me- knows all the different families. I can communicate with all

of them. No other viruses know how to communicate with one another.

46. I can even communicate with the ugly artificial amoebas; the man- made viruses; a blend of artificial chemicals.

47. You need to watch them like hawks, these amoebas. They are here to destroy you.

48. It's my job to be vigilant at all times and make sure I annihilate the bloody fuckers.

49. We are the viruses known to humans as germs. I do not like the word "germ". I devise the families of viruses into 2 groups and 10 sub- groups each.

50. The K1 group. K1-1, K1-2, K1-3, K1-4, K1-5, K1-6, K1-7, K1-8, K1-9.

51. The P1 group. P1-1, P1-2, P1-3, P1-4, P1-5, P1-6, P1-7, P1-8, P1-9.

52. The Amoebas come into 100 categories: A-1, A-2, A-3, A-4, A-5, A-6 until A-100.

ZONE A: ON THE OUTSIDE, ON THE SURFACE OF THE BODY.

The creature remembers. He sees an airport. He creates some associations.

Days of departure.

Days of arrival.

Check the time it takes.

Reloading.

Moving on.

Exhibit 5: OTHER GERMS

X1

ZONE B

53.   X1 is the master virus. There are also two other junior masters, also called X and X. We cannot meet.

54. If I ever meet other Xs, the game is over. X1 and X2 are only here as a back-up. If I would ever disappear, one of them would then take over and replace me and become the main master virus.

55. There must always be two junior masters. If one of the junior masters should ever replace the Master, a virus is randomly selected to become a junior master.

56. We, the viruses all live our lives in parallel and yet we all ignore each other. We have a purpose, an aim, a goal: to multiply and conquer.

57. Whilst all this is taking place inside a body,

on the outside it's even uglier -for the human that is-.

58. On the outside if we do a good job the animal agonises in pain, hallucinates and sometimes dies.

59. We aim to never kill a human. A human manages this task perfectly well. If the body dies we are forced to emigrate to another body. It is not very practical. Besides, having too many viruses is not a very good thing. It creates many conflicts with the ones already inside.

60. I was lucky. When I arrived, there was a shortage of one master virus. They needed me. When two master viruses meet, this means the end of the world. There can be only one master.

61. If there are two masters it means that there will be a war and the families of viruses will be forced to take sides.

62. Another cause for war can be triggered by chemicals inserted inside the body by other

humans.

63. War can also be declared by the amoebas when one of them decides that there should be a super amoeba.

64. I have never experienced more than 2 wars at the same time. To my knowledge, there have never been more than 2 wars at the same time. Three wars would be phenomenal. It would be apocalyptic.

65. The human or animal bodies are incredible machines. There's never a dull moment. Every second of the day -a day in human terms that is- is always different and never repeats itself.

ZONE A: ON THE OUTSIDE, ON THE SURFACE OF THE BODY

The human tries to enter into a new dimension. He believes he can float in the air.

The hallucination is brewing to the extreme.

He is nothing. He has nothing. He became a complete vegetable. The human is in a state of complete trance. The hallucination got the best of him.'

Exhibit 6: CONFLICT

X1

ZONE B

66. It is almost impossible to plan things from memory. The master and the junior viruses have a memory. No one else has got one.

67. Memory doesn't help. A memory is limited inside a body. Everything happens so instantly that the memory cannot work this fast.

68. Spontaneity is the key. There is no time to fuss about. We have to act accordingly and directly.

69. It has been a long while since anything serious happened. It is hard to divide and define our life inside a body. Once we're inside we rarely ever go out.

70. There is no sense of time. We could be

eating, copulating, infecting and travelling all at the same time.

71. We couldn't say that now we're doing this then later another thing. We cannot describe what we do or what we are.

72. We just exist and do things; backwards and in reverse, again and again in an endless loop. We never sleep or rest.

73. Although I have never had to use my memory since I moved in here, it does seem that for the past few minutes -in human terms- I have been immersed with a sinking feeling that things are moving in a direction not seen before.

74. There was this heavy pounding noise about. It must be really loud -in human terms- since a virus is deaf. Only the master virus can vaguely discern some noises.

75. Viruses cannot do the things humans do like smelling or seeing. Viruses have a very deep sense of feeling. They can feel anything, even from a distance.

76. I can feel that something isn't right. The heavy noise and some wind blowing from the top.

77. There is some white liquid flowing from the East End and some rather thick, sticky and transparent fluid barging in from the South.

78. I detect 100 rows of Super Amoebas skulking behind the transparent fluid. I detect more descending from the throat.

79. I beam -scream in human terms- to all the groups of viruses. I can reach every single one inside the body in an instant. The alarm has been raised: an attack has just started with a powerful force never encountered before.

80. Cohorts of viruses are gathering in rows of 100 000. Families are divided into legions. All viruses know what to do. They still need guidance and I can beam every single one accordingly. I can feel each part of this human body all at the same time. I'm the control centre.

ZONE A: ON THE OUTSIDE, ON THE SURFACE OF THE BODY

It's all wintry white.

It's solid white. It's the North Pole. It's like a giant dot shaping the horizon.

It's cold; icy cold and freezing. The human can barely move.

It's another zone. It's not a zone he has been through before. It's (definitively) a new dimension. It's the coldest weather on record.

It's silent. So silent...

Exhibit 7: HEART CONTROL

X1

ZONE B

81. I meet for the first time the 2 junior masters. We beam at each other. It can't be true! In the North there is another master virus and 2 junior viruses and another master in the East with no junior masters. It has never happened before. When I beam to my viruses I can reach them. When another master virus and his junior viruses intercept my beam, they get it all wrong.

82. I'm the oldest master virus and my viruses know this and obey me. However, the other master viruses will intercept my commands the wrong way. When there is an older master the powers of the other masters are somehow distorted. They can believe anything the Super Amoeba will tell them. They might even take

my viruses for families of super amoebas. The pounding noise is deafening.

83. This is it! It's war! A war of this kind has never happened before. It's gigantic. Fire!

I'm feeling more than myself, beyond myself. I'm everyone. I'm a human and yet I'm a germ, a virus.

Exhibit 8: WAR

X1

ZONE B

84. The War

1. Planning

Beam to all cohorts: fire to the enemy!

Beam to K-1: paralyse the liver

Beam to P-1: paralyse Master 2 located in the heart region moving South East and feed him to A-1

Beam to K-2: paralyse Master 3 located in the liver and feed him to A-2

Beam to K-3: paralyse Junior Masters located near Master 2 in the heart region moving South East and feed them to A-2

Beam to K-4: paralyse Junior Masters located

near Master 3 in the liver region and feed them to A-3

Beam to K-5: Assist K-1 and paralyse Master 2

Beam to K-6: Assist K-2 and paralyse Master 3

Beam to K-7: Assist K-3 and paralyse the Junior Masters 2

Beam to K-8: Assist K-4 and paralyse the Junior Masters 3

Beam to K-9: Rush the blood through the brain

Beam to P-2: Infect the spleen and rip it apart

Beam to P-3: You're near the transparent fluid: invade and procreate as fast as you can

Beam to P-4: Drag A-2 inside the transparent fluid and merge, procreate and ensure their full domination

Beam to P-5: Drag A-3 inside the transparent fluid and merge, procreate and ensure their full domination

Beam to P-6: Drag A-4 inside the transparent

fluid and merge, procreate and ensure their full domination

Beam to P-7: Drag A-5 inside the transparent fluid and merge, procreate and ensure their full domination

Beam to P-8: Drag A-6 inside the transparent fluid and merge, procreate and ensure their full domination

Beam to P-9: Rush over to me: I'm Southeast moving to the heart.

2. It is happening

Beam to K-5: Prepare to slaughter A-1

Beam to K-6: Engage with A-2 and paralyse the entire thorax region

Beam to K-7: Multiply in excess, spread and multiply the bloodstream

Beam to K-8: Fertilise the lungs region

Beam to K-9: Multiply and reproduce, again
and again until I say otherwise

ON THE OUTSIDE, ON THE SURFACE OF THE BODY

ZONE A

If anyone wonders what is happening on the
outside whilst a war is raging on the inside,
this is the time to talk about it. When one of my
cohorts reaches the brain, the result is almost
instant on the surface of the body; purple
circles of all sizes are recovering the whole
surface. When the liver is being copulated the
human screams and coughs incessantly.

When the heart is visited by 'Yours truly', the
human agonises in excruciating pain. This is
life on the surface of the body.

ZONE B

3. Battlefield 1

Beam to all the P cohorts: complete invasion of the fluid

4. Battlefield 2

Beam to all K cohorts: complete invasion of the blood stream

5. Battlefield 3

Beam to all: Attack!

Master to all: obey my orders!

6. Reload

7. Battlefield 4

Super A-8 and A-16 have swamped around K-6, K-7, K-8, K-9 and fertilised with a higher strain imaginable. I never had the A groups copulating in that way before. We have lost K-6, K-7, K-8, K-9. They have now become part of the A group.

K-1, K-2, K-3, K-4, K-5 have been fertilised by the A groups and conquered; each and one of them growing in millions of groups of viruses each.

8. Battlefield 5

Master 2 and his 2 junior masters have gained control of the North East and the South West.

P-1, P-2, P-3 have completely ignored my beams. They have submitted to Master 3.

A body cannot have 3 masters and junior masters but only one. If the other masters control all the cohorts, I'm done for!

9. Battlefield 6

Beam to all cohorts: I'm the ultimate master: surrender all your commands to me! I repeat: surrender all your commands to me!

Nothing doing: the battle is raging North, South, East and West in all the inner body's hemispheres.

My 2 junior masters have deserted me. Desertion! Desertion!

If this is the way it is going: prepare for total carnage! I repeat! Total carnage!

10. Game Over

Exhibit 9: ORGASM

X1

ZONE A: ON THE OUTSIDE, ON THE SURFACE OF THE BODY

Viruses reproduce almost in the same way as humans. We, viruses are what humans also call germs. We can also self-reproduce. It all depends what kind of virus we're after. Sometimes we need another virus. It depends on the strength of the species we want to create.

ZONE B

The war reaches the end. Reload.

85. The pounding from the heart is a nuclear bomb: it's exploding now; the body is being

ripped open. Hell! The guy is having open-heart surgery! Fucking hell! I'm being sucked out.

86. Beam P-9: rush over me now!

Beam K-9: leave the brain and rush over me!

87. Hell! Fuck! Help! I'm being flown through the blood, it's too fast! Where the hell? No! Not there, not through the mouth. Not the mouth! No! I've become a mouse again. A mouse! A stupid mortal mouse in the human world.

88. My life is over. Game Over. The End.

Exhibit 10: LEAVING

X1

ZONE A: ON THE OUTSIDE, ON THE SURFACE OF THE BODY

A cemetery, a tombstone; there are the last remnants of an earthling creature. The human contemplates the fact that he is about to die. He believes his time has come. What will happen after he's gone?

ZONE B

89. I was forced to leave a body where I was the one and only master.

90. Over a trillion viruses depended on me for their survival.

91. I have been banished from a place where I believed I would be alive for as long as the body would live.

92. One day, the power that be, forced me out. How fast can a whole population switch its allegiance from one master to another?

93. A mouse can still yield unwavering powers into the outside world and a mouth is the ultimate gate control.

94. It has never been in the interest of a virus or a germ to kill. When a body dies, the viruses die with it.

95. Inside the body I was somebody but on the outside. I'm a 'nobody'. One can only be a 'somebody' once.

96. I may not have been exactly who I thought I had been. I might have been just a simple dot floating into space.

97. X2 and X1, the two humans inside the taxi were just two miserable dots. We're all dots dotting the horizon; a dot with an imagination creating colours out of an empty space.

ZONE A

Inside the cab, X1 and X2

X2

I can't take it anymore from this book!

X2 storms out of the cab and disappears into the night.

X1

98. The story is proving too much for him. What is most puzzling with this story even to me is that X2 became too bewildered by it. He thought it was a story about him.   Even inside a book, on the outside my influence knows no bounds.

99. The virus has caught up with them and the story became their story. They have been reading their very own story. Funny how can anyone believe they can be someone, somewhere when in reality they are not! The imagination in every creature is so powerful

that it can erase someone's own memory.

100. The very end. **Reload and restart!**

1010101010101010101010101010101010101010